I SURVIVED

THE BATTLE OF D-DAY, 1944

by **Lauren Tarshis**

illustrated by **Scott Dawson**

Scholastic Inc.

Text copyright © 2019 by Dreyfuss Tarshis Media, Inc.

Illustrations copyright © 2019 by Scholastic Inc.

Photos ©: iv: National Archives and Records Administration; 115, 116: Author's collection; 121: Keystone-France/Getty Images; 125: National Archives and Records Administration; 126: Universal History Archive/Getty Images; 127: National Archives and Records Administration; 130: Military History Collection/Alamy Stock Photo; 131: Roger Viollet/Getty Images; 133: National Archives and Records Administration.

Special thanks to Edgar F. Raines, Jr.

This book is being published simultaneously in hardcover by Scholastic Press.

ISBN 978-1-338-31738-1

10 9   21 22 23

Printed in the U.S.A.   40
First printing 2019
Designed by Yaffa Jaskoll and Heather Daugherty

For Marilyn Merker Goldman

CHAPTER 1

TUESDAY, JUNE 6, 1944
THE CLIFFS ABOVE OMAHA BEACH
NORMANDY, FRANCE
AROUND 1:00 A.M.

Eleven-year-old Paul Colbert was running for his life.

It was D-Day, one of the bloodiest days of World War II. More than 150,000 soldiers from America, England, and Canada were invading France.

They had sailed across the sea on seven thousand ships, creeping through the dark of night.

Their mission: to free France from the brutal grip of Nazi Germany. It was time to crush the Nazis, and end the war.

In the minutes before the ships arrived, Paul was crouched on a cliff above the beach. He was trying to escape before the battle began. But now warplanes were zooming through the sky. And suddenly there was a shattering blast.

Kaboom!

Paul looked up in horror and saw that a plane was now in flames. And it was in a fiery death spiral, heading right for him.

Paul ran wildly as the burning plane fell from the sky. The air filled with the gagging stench of burning metal and melting rubber. The engine screamed and moaned. It sounded like a giant beast bellowing in pain.

No matter where Paul went, the dying plane seemed to be following him, like it wanted Paul to die, too.

And then, *smack!* Something hit Paul on the head. His skull seemed to explode in pain. Paul fell to the ground as the burning wreckage came crashing down.

For four long years, Paul had been praying for this day — for the war to end, for France to be finally free from the Nazis.

But now, it seemed, this day would be his last.

CHAPTER 2

Paul kicked his soccer ball along the winding dirt road. For the first time in months, he wasn't worrying about the miserable war. He wasn't wondering whether he'd ever see Papa again. He wasn't thinking about Adolf Hitler, the evil German Nazi leader, or his soldiers who'd invaded Paul's country, his town, and his life.

This is going to be a good day, he told himself. It was his mother's birthday. Paul was going to buy her some cookies.

How long had it been since he or his mother — Maman — had eaten a cookie or a cake or a bar of chocolate? He had no idea. With the war in its fifth year, all the best foods had disappeared. Poor Maman made her coffee out of ground acorns mixed with hot water.

Paul's mouth watered as he remembered biting into a chocolate éclair, with the sweet, velvety cream that slid down his throat. Or a crepe filled with strawberry jam that made his fingers sticky all day.

Maman's favorites were madeleines, little buttery cookies that melted in your mouth. So that's what Paul would get for her.

Paul pictured Maman now — her gentle eyes, her warm smile. She worked all the time, sewing and mending clothing to support them. Some mornings she was gone making deliveries before he climbed out of bed.

Making Maman happy was worth anything to Paul.

Even his soccer ball.

He gave the brown leather ball a gentle tap with his toe.

That's how he was going to get Maman her cookies. He would sell the ball. Right now he was heading to the dingy little market down by the river. That's where desperate people from Le Roc went to sell things — their wedding rings, their prized books, their last pair of shoes.

Nobody played much soccer these days. Practically every young man in Europe was either fighting in the war or was a prisoner of the Germans. But Paul's soccer ball was leather, which was scarce. Someone could cut it up and turn it into a pair of shoes or gloves.

Paul flinched as he imagined his ball getting butchered. He kicked it even more gently.

Maman and Papa had given it to him for his seventh birthday. He'd rushed over to show it to his best friend, Gerard. They were both soccer fanatics.

"Now we're going to the World Cup for sure!" Gerard had said, pushing his curls out of his eyes and cracking that bright, lopsided smile of his.

Over the next few years, this ball had gone everywhere with them.

They'd chased it thousands of times across their schoolyard. They'd dribbled it through the wheat fields and orchards and down every cobble-stoned street of their town. They'd practiced penalty kicks on the beach as the waves crashed, diving into the sand to stop the ball from rolling into the ocean.

"Race you!" Paul would shout, and he and Gerard would go charging after the ball.

Paul still loved the game. But he hadn't touched the soccer ball in months.

Not since Gerard had disappeared.

The Nazis had taken Gerard and his family away.

Paul's stomach twisted as he thought about it. One cold night in March, the Nazis had arrested every Jewish person in town and shoved them into trucks. Nobody knew for sure where the

Nazis had taken them, but there were rumors too horrifying to believe. About children torn away from their parents. About train cars where people were packed so tightly they couldn't breathe. About huge prisons where people were starved and worked to death.

Some nights Paul lay in his bed, praying that what he'd heard wasn't true.

Paul gave his ball a furious kick. Then he closed his eyes and took a breath. *No,* he told himself. He wasn't going to think about the Nazis today. It was Maman's birthday.

This was going to be a good day.

CHAPTER 3

ONE HOUR LATER

Paul brushed off his soccer ball one last time, then slapped it on the table at the market.

"I'm not taking that," the man behind the table said gruffly. Paul knew his name was Boris. He was the only leatherworker left in town. "Nobody wants one of those," Boris said.

Paul scrunched up his face, trying to think of what to say to Boris next.

"But it's good leather," Paul said.

Boris shook his head. "Don't want it."

Paul sighed. He hadn't thought of what would happen if he couldn't sell the ball. He grabbed it back and found a quiet spot in the dirt to sit down and think.

This park near the river used to be a place filled with flowers, where families sat on blankets and ate crunchy bread and soft cheese. Where kids threw their bread crusts to the ducks and floated toy sailboats in the river.

There were no flowers anymore, no food for picnics. The Nazis had chopped down the trees and sent the wood to Germany. Nobody came here for fun. Even the ducks were gone; people had eaten them out of desperation.

But Paul had an extra reason for hating it down here. It was something that had happened last fall. Paul picked up a stick and stabbed it into the dirt as the memory flashed through his mind like a jagged piece of glass.

He'd come here with Maman that day, to sell the last of the silver cups she'd inherited from her grandmother. They had to sell the cup to buy coal for the winter so they wouldn't freeze. Paul was waiting for Maman as she bargained with the merchant who bought silver. And then suddenly Paul saw a man walking very quickly across the park.

Paul instantly recognized him: It was his teacher, Mr. Leon.

Paul and Gerard loved Mr. Leon. He never yelled at them when they kicked their ball through the hall. He told the best stories about the Castle Le Roc, the crumbling old castle at the edge of town. He told them that many believed there was a dragon that still lived in the tower. It was a huge winged beast with a snake's head, a falcon beak, and fiery breath.

"Its glowing eyes peer through the cracks of the tower," he would say, in that low, smooth voice of his. "Its wings go *whoosh, whoosh, whoosh*!"

Most people in town were too scared to go to the castle. But sometimes Paul and Gerard would sneak up there.

But even better than his stories, Mr. Leon made Paul feel safe. No matter what was happening outside their school.

That day in the park, Paul was about to call out

to Mr. Leon. But suddenly Mr. Leon broke into a run. And two Nazi soldiers came chasing after him.

Paul closed his eyes, trying to stop the nightmare memory — the three gunshots, the sight of Mr. Leon falling to the ground and then rolling into the river. Paul had watched as his teacher's body sank down. Even now, he couldn't believe that Mr. Leon was gone.

Paul stabbed the dirt with the stick again. He remembered how the Nazis closed down the school after that. They said Mr. Leon was a traitor, a criminal, and a spy.

But as it turned out, Mr. Leon was a hero.

What nobody had known before Mr. Leon's murder was that he belonged to a secret group called the resistance.

It was like a small army, but not with soldiers. Its members were regular people — writers, shopkeepers, farmers, doctors . . . and teachers. They stole Nazi secrets for the Allies. They blew up Nazi trains loaded with weapons and tanks. It still shocked Paul that Mr. Leon had been in the resistance.

It didn't matter now, though. The resistance had been crushed, in Le Roc and all over France. That's what Paul had heard. The Nazis had hunted the members down, killed thousands of them. And usually the Nazis didn't just shoot them. They tortured them first so they would spill the names of others in their group.

Mr. Leon, people said, had been lucky he died quickly.

Paul closed his eyes. Mr. Leon had risked his life fighting for something important. Couldn't Paul at least try a little harder to get a present for Maman? He couldn't give up so easily.

Back at Boris's table, Paul set the ball down once again.

"I told you," Boris said, his lips closing in a tight line. "Nobody wants that ball. Take it home."

Paul felt a lump forming in his throat.

"Please . . . it's my mother's birthday," he said, struggling to keep his voice steady. "I need the money so I can get her a gift."

Without a word, Boris snatched the ball. He reached into his pocket and handed Paul ten coins.

Paul's heart leaped. He smiled at Boris, then took the coins and ran to the bakery, the one all the Nazi officers went to.

Paul slapped his coins on the counter. The pretty, young shopgirl, Marie, looked at him with surprise.

"One dozen madeleines please," he said.

Five minutes later, Paul had one dozen cookies warm from the oven, tucked into a little white box.

He walked home along the dirt road. He breathed in the sweet, buttery smell.

Maman had said she wouldn't be home until late tonight, after Paul went to bed. But the cookies would stay fresh until then. Paul pictured Maman's smiling face when she took her first bite.

Suddenly the air filled with the ferocious roar of engines.

Vroom! Vroom!

Paul whipped around just as a swarm of Nazi soldiers on motorcycles came zooming around the corner.

They were heading right for him.

CHAPTER 4

Paul threw himself out of the way and smashed into the wall of thick, towering bushes that lined the road. He held his breath. The soldiers zoomed by. They were a blur of gray metal and black leather and red Nazi flags.

Those soldiers would have run him down, Paul knew. They would have crushed him under speeding wheels and left him for dead. Like a worm cut in two by a plow.

Where were those soldiers going? The question stabbed him in the gut. He knew that somebody was about to get arrested — or shot.

Paul pulled himself out of the thick, prickly bushes and stared at the cookies — or what little was left of them.

The box lay open a few feet away in front of a gate in the hedge. The cookies were smashed to pieces. Paul desperately tried to scoop up the crumbs.

But it was useless.

Hot tears stung his eyes.

He hated those men! He wanted to chase them down, knock them off their bikes, rip away those swastika flags and stamp them under his boots.

Of course Paul couldn't do that. All he could do was sit here in the road, crying like a baby over a pile of cookie crumbs. But Paul knew that wasn't what was truly bothering him.

It was this helpless feeling. There was nothing he could do to fight back against the Nazis.

Nothing *anyone* could do.

Papa had tried to fight back . . . and look what had happened to him.

He'd joined the French army right after Germany invaded France. Within six weeks, the

Germans had killed tens of thousands of French soldiers. They took nearly two million men prisoner, including Papa. France surrendered. Now the Nazi flag flapped over the Eiffel Tower — and most of Europe, too.

And Papa? He was trapped in a Nazi prison camp somewhere in Germany. Paul and Maman hadn't heard from him in four years.

Paul shook his head to clear his mind. He couldn't just sit here crying all day.

He was brushing off his trousers when he heard a strange sound.

"Coo-roo."

He looked up, and a plump gray bird was staring at him from the bushes. The bird swooped through the air and landed at Paul's feet.

It must have come for the cookies.

"Go ahead," Paul said, motioning to the crumbs. "Someone should eat them."

But the bird ignored the crumbs. It peered up at Paul. It had very shiny eyes, gold with a dot of black in the middle.

"*Coo-roo,*" it said brightly. "*Coo-roo, coo-roo, coo-roo.*"

It fluffed its feathers at Paul. And then it flew around in a slow circle, hovering for a moment right in front of his face.

"*Coo-roo.*"

"What?" Paul asked gently. "What do you want?"

Was he actually talking to a pigeon?

Yes. And the pigeon seemed to be talking to him.

"*Coo-roo.*"

The bird took off over the hedge into the meadow. And Paul walked through the gate after it. It had been a bad morning. Following a friendly bird into a meadow didn't seem like such a bad idea.

The bird flew low, looped around Paul, and headed for a tall apple tree in the middle of the meadow. It circled the tree as Paul walked through the tall grass to join it. Then, all of a sudden, the bird zipped up into the leaves and Paul lost sight of it.

He gazed up through the branches, searching for the bird.

Something wet dropped onto Paul's head. He wiped it away and glanced at his hand.

It was streaked with blood.

He cautiously stepped aside, and looked up. Paul froze at what he saw.

His mouth fell open but he was too shocked to scream.

CHAPTER 5

High up in the tree, dangling from a branch, was a man in a dark-green army uniform. Paul couldn't see him from this angle very well. But he knew the man was a soldier. He was attached to the tree by the strings of a parachute, which must have snagged on one of the upper branches. Paul had no doubt the man was dead.

Based on his uniform, Paul guessed the soldier was American or British, or maybe Canadian. Those countries were Hitler's enemies. They had banded together with Russia and other countries, and were fighting against Germany in the war. They had formed a team: the Allies.

This soldier must have flown here from one of the air bases in England. That's where the Allies had most of their soldiers and bases now. England was one of the only countries in Europe the Nazis hadn't been able to swallow up. All that separated France from England was a narrow slice of ocean, called the English Channel.

Paul tried to get a better look. He stepped slowly, his boots crunching in the grass.

He used to dream that the Allies would rescue France. But he'd given up on that a long time ago. The Nazis were too strong. They had France all locked up. The beaches here in Le Roc and along the coast were lined with cannons and machine guns.

Allied planes sometimes made it through to drop bombs. But just as often their planes were shot down over France. Their soldiers sometimes escaped — they bailed out and parachuted to the ground. That's what must have happened to this soldier. But then he'd crashed into this tree . . . and died.

"Hey, kid, can you help me?" a voice called down.

Paul jumped so high he nearly hit his head on a branch. So this soldier *wasn't* dead. He spoke in French, but with a strange twang. American, maybe?

"I need to cut myself down from here, but I dropped my knife," the soldier continued. "It's somewhere on the ground."

Paul scanned the grass. There it was, a sharp-looking knife with a wooden handle.

Paul took a step toward it, but then his body froze.

A terrified little voice shouted inside his skull.

Are you crazy?! Stop right now! Get out of here quick!

Paul knew what happened to people who were caught helping Allied soldiers.

A couple months ago, the Nazis had found an Allied pilot hiding in a barn near the edge of town. They shot the pilot and the farmer who owned the barn. They sent that farmer's family — including his little children — to a work camp. Nobody expected them to make it out of there alive.

Run! Get away from here, the little voice whispered in Paul's mind.

"Hey, kid," the man called. "It will just take a minute."

Paul blocked out the voice in his skull. Instead, he thought of Papa behind barbed wire. He thought of Gerard, being shoved into a truck.

24

He thought of Mr. Leon. And he thought of that friendly little pigeon that seemed to have led him to this exact spot.

Before Paul even knew what he was doing, he'd snatched the knife from the grass.

He tucked it into the waistband of his trousers and started climbing up the tree.

CHAPTER 6

Paul climbed quickly. He felt like he was being pulled along by some invisible force, like he was a nail moving toward a magnet.

He made it up to the soldier, and handed over the knife. The man looked young, maybe twenty-five or so. He wasn't tall, but muscles bulged under his uniform. He seemed very strong.

"Thanks, kid," he said, flashing a smile.

He had one of those faces that was bright and open and made you feel like you'd known him a long time.

"You're welcome," Paul said, trying not to stare too hard.

The soldier's uniform was covered with pockets. Pouches and bags of different sizes and shapes were strapped to his chest, his arms, and his legs. Paul spotted a tear in his pants and a nasty gash on his shin. That must have been where the blood had come from.

"My name's Victor," the soldier said, eyeing Paul as he sliced through one of the shoulder straps of his parachute harness. "Sergeant Victor Lopez, American army."

So Paul had guessed right.

"Who are you?" Victor asked.

"Paul," he answered.

Paul noticed the small silver pin on the collar of Victor's uniform. It showed a parachute between a set of wings. And Paul understood. This man hadn't parachuted down because his plane had crashed. He'd jumped out. There were soldiers trained to do that, Paul knew. They were called paratroopers.

"How long have you been up here?" Paul asked.

"Since about four A.M. Wasn't a good flight. We came under enemy fire coming off the English Channel. Plane barely got me here. I had to jump out way too low, no time to steer. So I wound up stuck in this tree."

"*Coo-roo.*"

Paul's head snapped up. There was that friendly pigeon again, perched on the branch right above Victor.

"That's Ellie," Victor said, cutting the last string of the parachute. He dropped down to take a seat on the branch next to Paul and shook his head at the bird. "I told you to get going."

He looked at Paul. "Ellie's a carrier pigeon."

Those were pigeons that carried messages, Paul knew. Paul noticed the little metal tube attached to the bird's leg. That's where you could put a rolled-up piece of paper.

"They sent her along with me," Victor continued. "She's supposed to fly back to England with a message so people know I got stuck in this tree. But she doesn't seem to want to leave me."

"I think she likes you," Paul said.

Ellie gazed at Victor with her shiny gold eyes. *In love* was more like it.

"The army's going to fire you, Ellie," Victor said.

"Coo-roo," Ellie answered.

Paul laughed without meaning to. The sound — his own low chuckle — was one he hadn't heard much lately.

Victor cracked a smile and shook his head.

Paul had about a million questions he wanted to ask.

The most important: What was Victor doing here in Le Roc?

But then he heard the sound of a motor.

Paul looked out to the road and saw a Nazi patrol truck creeping slowly along. The truck stopped right near the gate that led into the meadow.

Paul and Victor both scrambled down the tree. They glanced around, but the whole meadow was surrounded by those thick, tall bushes. Those bushes — they were called hedgerows — were everywhere in this part of France.

But Paul knew they weren't always as solid as they looked. He and Gerard used to play soccer here. They were always crawling through the hedgerows to find their lost ball. Paul spotted a good hiding place just up ahead.

"There!" Paul said, dashing over to the spot. He pulled some vines aside.

"Good work," Victor whispered as they both crawled in. Ellie flew in behind them.

They were well hidden now — and just in time.

Four German soldiers appeared through the gate.

Paul's eyes narrowed as he recognized the tall man leading the way.

It was Captain Egon Stroop. He was a monster, the cruelest Nazi in Le Roc, for sure. He had personally led the roundup of the Jewish people this past March. Paul's neighbors said Stroop had used a whip to force them into trucks, smiling the entire time.

Of course Stroop had his dog with him now, a wolflike German shepherd. It was a trained killer, Paul had heard, with jaws strong enough to crack a human skull.

Paul shivered, even though it was warm outside.

The Nazis circled the tree, looking up at Victor's parachute.

But the dog was racing around sniffing the ground. Suddenly it stopped. Right in the spot where Paul had first spotted Victor.

The blood, thought Paul. *It smells Victor's blood.*

The dog lifted its head. Its nose twitched. Its fur stood up. Its lips peeled back to show a row of gleaming white fangs. With a burst of speed, the snarling beast came charging toward them.

CHAPTER 7

Paul stayed still as a stone. He tried not to imagine that dog's teeth tearing into his neck, cracking his bones.

There was a rustling in the leaves above him. What looked like a feathered gray bullet shot out from the bushes toward the dog.

It was Ellie!

She flew up to the dog, gave it a vicious peck on the nose, and then landed on its back.

The dog stopped short and yelped in fear. Ellie took off again, flying around the dog like a tiny fighter plane, flapping her wings. She let out a clucking shriek — a pigeon battle cry.

The dog leaped up, snapping and growling, its jaws foaming. But Ellie didn't fly away. Either she was the bravest pigeon that ever lived, or the craziest. The Nazis came running over, with Stroop in the lead. They were close enough now so that Paul could see Stroop's face — the white, waxy skin; the thin, crooked lips; and the watery, yellowed eyes.

Paul's gut filled with a sickening churn of hatred and fear.

Stroop gripped his machine gun and aimed it at Ellie.

Brrrrrrt! Brrrrrrt! Bullets sprayed through the air.

Stroop missed Ellie. But now his dog was whining and crying in terror. It turned and went charging across the meadow and through the gate.

Stroop screamed out some furious German words, which sent the other three Nazis on a mad dash after the dog.

Paul looked for Ellie, but she'd flown off.

Stroop stood there, looking around. Then he stamped his foot and rushed after them. For now, it seemed nothing was more important than finding his dog.

Paul and Victor crawled out of the bushes. They stared at each other in relief, but they knew that Stroop would be back.

"Is there another way out of here?" Victor asked.

Paul nodded. He led Victor down to the corner of the meadow, through a gap in the bushes and into an apple orchard. But this wasn't safe, either. Someone could easily spot Victor and report him. There were people in town — dirty rats — who spied for the Nazis in exchange for money and food.

Paul's heart hammered.

Ellie appeared, and landed at Paul's feet.

"Coo-roo," she said.

"Think!" she seemed to be saying.

And then it came to Paul — the one place where Victor might just be safe.

"I know where you can hide," Paul said. "And I can take you there."

Victor shook his head. "No, Paul. You need to get home. This is way too much to ask . . ."

But suddenly they heard shouting voices.

German voices.

There was no time to argue.

They took off.

Paul led Victor through the orchard. It was surrounded by hedgerows. But Paul knew a spot where they could cut through into a wheat field. They ran through the feathery stalks and scaled a stone wall.

As they zigzagged across Le Roc, Paul kept thinking of Gerard. They'd explored every inch of this town. There wasn't a secret path they hadn't discovered. Paul heard Gerard's voice echoing in his mind. *Race you!* Paul ran faster.

Finally, after one last turn, there it was: the one place in town where nobody would go. Not even the Nazis.

The Castle Le Roc.

It was exactly as Paul remembered — the

crumbling walls, the filthy blackened stones, the green vines crawling up to the windows, like thousands of twisting snakes. The tower rose up crookedly into the sky.

"What is this place?" Victor asked.

"It's an old castle," Paul said. "Nobody ever comes here."

"I can see why," Victor answered.

Paul didn't mention the dragon. And he especially didn't mention the creepy story he'd heard last summer. People said that a burned body had been found at the base of the tower. The police had searched the property but still had no idea who — or what — had killed the person.

Paul wasn't sure what to make of that story. But this much he knew: The castle was creepier than ever. It was the perfect place for Victor to hide.

Ellie swooped down and landed next to Victor.

Paul wondered how she'd do against a dragon.

Just then there were footsteps behind them.

Paul turned as a masked man with a rifle leaped out from behind a tree.

CHAPTER 8

"Don't move!" the man shouted.

He pointed a rifle at Victor's chest.

He wasn't a Nazi; he was speaking French, and was wearing regular clothes. Paul had no idea who he could be. He wore a blue scarf across his face, like a bandit — or a murderer.

Paul's heart stopped.

He must be working for the Nazis!

He'd collect a big reward for catching Victor. And Paul? He'd get extra for him.

Victor tried to talk to him. "My name is —"

"Shut up!" the man said, his eyes darting all around. "Is anyone else with you?"

"No," Victor said.

"You better hope so. Now move it!" the man said.

Before Paul knew it, they'd been shoved through the front door of the castle, pushed down a long, cold, and dark hallway, and thrown into a room.

The door slammed shut. Paul's teeth were chattering, and not because it was cold in there.

A foul smell of dead mice and centuries of rot rose up.

If this wasn't a dungeon, Paul didn't know what it was. It felt haunted.

But right now he wasn't afraid of any dragon or ghosts.

All he could imagine was Stroop's yellowed eyes and smiling face when he shoved Gerard into the back of a truck.

"Paul," Victor said quietly. "Stay calm. I think I know who that man is."

"You do?"

"I think he's in the resistance."

"The resistance?" Paul asked. "I thought the Nazis killed them all."

Victor shook his head.

"No, Paul. There are still thousands left."

"But aren't we on the same side?"

"Yes," Victor said. "But they can't trust anyone. We may have stumbled into some kind of resistance hideout."

"This castle?"

"It makes sense, doesn't it?" Victor said. "You said it yourself. It's the one place the Nazis won't go."

Paul was afraid to feel hopeful, but then the door swung open. Standing there was a tall man with wild gray hair, glasses, and a thick mustache.

Paul's knees went weak. It couldn't be . . . could it?

Mr. Leon was supposed to be dead.

CHAPTER 9

Mr. Leon looked equally stunned.

Victor's voice broke the silence.

"I'm Sergeant Victor Lopez," he said. "American army. And this boy here is — "

Mr. Leon stepped forward and grabbed Paul into a crushing hug.

And now it was Victor's turn to be shocked.

Paul held his teacher tight, fighting back tears.

"We're old friends," Mr. Leon told Victor when he and Paul finally stepped apart. Mr. Leon took off his round glasses and wiped away his own tears. He put his glasses back on and held his hand out to Victor.

"A pleasure to finally meet you, Sergeant Lopez," he said in that deep, cheerful voice that Paul knew so well.

But wait. How did Mr. Leon know who Victor was?

"Welcome to the headquarters of the Le Roc resistance," he said.

Victor had been right!

"I know why the Allies sent you," Mr. Leon continued. "We are ready to help you with this mission. We had our people out looking for you last night. But they couldn't find you."

Paul turned to Victor. A mission? With the resistance? That's why Victor had come to Le Roc?

It seemed so.

"I would have been captured," Victor said. "If it hadn't been for Paul."

He told Mr. Leon how Paul had climbed the tree, how he'd helped Victor escape.

"This kid is brave," he said.

"I've always known that," Mr. Leon said proudly. But then his eyebrows pressed together with worry.

"Paul, how did you possibly know to come here? Did you know that this was a resistance base? Did you have any idea that I —"

"No, sir!" Paul exclaimed. "I thought nobody would be here. And, Mr. Leon, I was there when you got shot. I thought you . . ."

He stared at his teacher, and it all came back — those three shots. The screams. The sight of Mr. Leon's lifeless body sinking into the river.

Paul's throat tightened, and he looked down at the dusty stone floor.

"I'm sorry, Paul," Mr. Leon said softly. "I wish I could have let you know that I was all right. But only a few people know that I escaped. If the Nazis had caught me, it would have put the lives of many people in danger. It's far better that the Nazis believe I'm at the bottom of that river."

Paul didn't doubt that.

"Victor," Mr. Leon said, "let's get you settled so we can get to work."

Mr. Leon led them out of the room.

Someone was waiting for them.

"Coo-roo."

"She's my carrier pigeon," Victor told Mr. Leon.

"Excellent!" Mr. Leon said. "She can send a message back that you've made it."

Victor and Paul eyed each other. They'd tell Mr. Leon about Ellie later. That pigeon wasn't going anywhere.

Mr. Leon introduced them to Pierre, the man who'd dragged them in here. He wasn't wearing his mask anymore. Paul recognized him. He was a policeman in town.

"Sorry for the rough welcome," Pierre said, giving Paul's shoulder a squeeze.

Paul understood why Pierre had been so protective. But he also knew Pierre's old rifle wouldn't do much good if the Nazis raided this place. Hopefully the legend of the dragon would keep the Nazis away. And if that didn't do it, the story of the burned body should scare them off.

Victor and the men disappeared down the winding hall, with Ellie fluttering behind.

Now Mr. Leon and Paul were alone.

"Paul," his teacher said. "It's not safe for you to leave here now. I know the Nazis are searching everywhere for Sergeant Lopez. And someone might have spotted you in that area. We need to find out exactly what the Nazis know. So I want you to stay here."

Paul's skin tingled. He *wanted* to stay. But then he thought of Maman.

"What about my mother?" Paul asked. He couldn't just not come home. She'd be frantic with worry.

"About your mother," Mr. Leon said. "She's due here in just a couple hours."

He spoke slowly, like when he was explaining a math problem that wasn't as simple as it looked. It took a moment for the meaning of Mr. Leon's words to sink in.

"Maman?" Paul said. "Is she . . . is she in the resistance?"

How was that possible?

Maman? Quiet, gentle Maman?

Mr. Leon nodded. "She's one of many people in Le Roc who are a part of this fight. She's one of our best messengers."

Paul thought of all those mornings when Maman left on her bicycle before dawn. When she got home late, her face flushed, peering out the curtains as she fixed supper.

Paul felt that his world had suddenly cracked open. And inside was another world, a world filled with dangerous secrets. More dangerous than Paul could imagine.

"I know your mother wanted to keep you as far as possible from all this," Mr. Leon said. "But you found your way here anyway."

Waves of feelings sloshed through Paul's head and heart.

There was fear. Because Paul thought of the thousands of people in the resistance who had been caught — men, women, and teenagers.

There was some anger — how many lies had Maman told Paul over the years?

46

But the feelings that rose up inside Paul, brighter than all the others, were hope and pride.

Mr. Leon was alive. The people of Le Roc hadn't given up. They were fighting back! Maman was part of the resistance!

Paul stood up taller.

"Mr. Leon," he said. "Please let me help."

CHAPTER 10

FIVE HOURS LATER

"As we all know, the Nazis are hiding the weapons right here," Mr. Leon said, pointing to a spot on the map. "They're in the old barn they've been using as a warehouse."

Paul was sitting next to Victor in a room in the castle basement. The small room was crowded. Throughout the afternoon, more people had arrived.

And Paul had been shocked to discover that he recognized every one of them.

There was Marie, the young woman who had served him the cookies at the bakery. Her work at the shop made her one of the resistance's most prized spies. She'd picked up many secrets listening while the Nazi soldiers gorged themselves on cakes and tarts.

There was Mr. Spire, an older man with a limp, who'd been friends with Paul's grandfather. Pierre the policeman was back. And there was Mrs. Bernard, a gray-haired woman who had the prettiest voice in the church choir.

Paul would never have guessed any of these people would be in the resistance. And of course the person he'd least suspected was sitting next to him.

Maman.

She'd arrived a couple hours ago. Mr. Leon had spoken to her first; then she came to find Paul. They'd sat for a moment alone, holding hands, wiping away tears. But not much needed to be said. Now Paul knew all about Maman's secret life. And whether Maman liked it or not, Paul was a part of it.

And anyway, there was no time for tearful talk.

Mr. Leon had gathered them to discuss an urgent mission, the one that Victor had come to Le Roc to help with. The Nazis were keeping some deadly weapons in Le Roc. These weapons needed to be destroyed.

"The Allies have sent us another message," Mr. Leon went on. "They want these terrible weapons destroyed *tonight*."

It was Maman who had brought this message, Paul had learned. There were people in town who'd been given secret radios they used to communicate with the Allies. One of Maman's jobs was to pick up those messages and deliver them to other resistance members in and around Le Roc.

"These are one of the Nazis' most powerful weapons," said Mr. Spire. "More destructive than anything I remember from World War One." He'd actually fought in that war with Paul's grandfather. "They can kill one thousand men in minutes."

A chill went up Paul's spine. Victor had told him about these weapons earlier. They were a kind of powerful cannon with six barrels. Each one could shoot one hundred exploding rockets in a minute. The weapon was called a *Nebelwerfer,* a German word that Paul didn't understand. But he knew it must mean something evil. When the rockets hit, they exploded, killing everything in their path. This made *Nebelwerfers* one of the most feared weapons the Nazis had.

"The Allies have told us that this mission is urgent," Mr. Leon said. "That's why they took the unusual step of sending Victor. He is one of their best men. Victor is not simply a soldier. He is a special agent, trained in explosives."

Victor nodded, and now Mr. Leon stepped aside so Victor could take over. Victor stood up and explained that the mission should be simple.

"I have brought a new kind of plastic explosive. It's called C-Three."

He lifted a block of what looked like dull yellow clay.

"This explosive is very light. Just a small amount will cause a powerful blast. We can slice off a bit and put it in one of the cannon barrels.

Once the Nazis try to fire the cannon, the whole thing will explode."

"We will turn their weapon of death against them," said Mrs. Bernard.

Paul eyed her, surprised to hear these harsh words coming from the same mouth that sang their Christmas carols.

"Exactly," said Victor.

"Any questions?" Mr. Leon asked.

He leaned forward and looked at each person, one by one. It was the same look he used at school, the one that made Paul feel a little smarter. Like suddenly he could accomplish anything he set his mind to.

"I have a question," Marie said, putting down her mug of cider. "We informed the Allies that there were *Nebelwerfers* here months ago. Now they've sent Victor and we must destroy these weapons tonight. What changed to make things so urgent?"

The others murmured their agreement, and Maman nodded her head. Paul had been wondering the same thing.

Mr. Leon glanced at Victor, who looked down. Paul sensed there was something they weren't sharing with the rest of the group.

Mr. Spire put his hand over Mr. Leon's. "Jacques," he said. "Are the Allies about to attack France? Is the invasion about to happen? Is that why they want the weapons destroyed?"

"Are the Allies coming here, to Normandy?" Pierre chimed in.

The room seemed to shimmer, though nobody moved.

Mr. Leon was still for a moment. And then he slowly nodded.

"The day has finally come," he said softly. "I don't know everything; this is still top secret. If the Germans find out, the invasion will almost certainly fail. I can tell you that the Allies are sending a massive force across the English Channel. This will be the largest invasion by sea in the history of the world — thousands of ships. They will arrive at dawn. Tens of thousands of men will be coming ashore on the beaches of Normandy, including right here in Le Roc."

LONDON

ENGLAND

English

UTAH OMAHA GOLD JUNO SWORD

NORMANDY BEACHES

FRAN

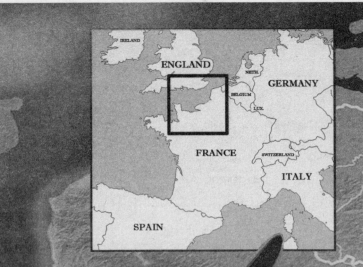

Paul held his breath. The largest invasion in history?

Mr. Leon paused and looked around. "I don't have to tell you what those *Nebelwerfers* could do to those men trying to come onto the beaches. It will be a slaughter."

Marie and Pierre both leaped to their feet.

They turned to Victor.

"Let's go," said Marie. "We must destroy the weapons tonight!"

CHAPTER 11

The hours crept by.

Paul sat in the radio room with Maman, Mr. Spire, Mrs. Bernard, and Mr. Leon.

Victor, Pierre, and Marie had left the moment it was dark. Victor said they should be back within two hours.

Paul watched the clock on the table.

Maman and Mrs. Bernard sat in front of the radio. Mrs. Bernard spun a bicycle wheel that powered the radio. There was no electricity in the castle, of course. Their light came sputtering from just a couple candles set up by the far wall.

They couldn't have them near the windows for fear of the Nazis seeing the flickers. Their supper — bread and stewed onions — was cold.

The radio was tuned to the BBC, the London station. That's how the Allies sent many of their most important messages to the resistance. Mr. Leon said a new message was coming soon. But right now there was music playing. The jolly sounds of pianos and horns brightened their dim and chilly room.

Paul kept rushing to the window, to peer up at the sky. Mr. Leon had explained that the Allies would be sending thousands and thousands of paratroopers ahead of the ships. These soldiers would keep German troops from getting to the beach to fight the Allies.

"See anything yet?" Mr. Spire asked him.

Paul shook his head. The only thing coming from the sky right now was a light, spitting rain.

"The paratroopers won't arrive until after midnight," Mr. Leon said. "And I don't know if any are coming this close to the beaches."

Paul kept watch anyway. He just wanted a sign that this invasion was real and not just a dream.

An hour crept by. Two.

Paul was so restless he didn't know what to do with himself.

"Paul," Mr. Leon said finally. "Come sit."

Maman smiled up at him as he passed. She was tailoring a jacket for one of her customers, a reminder that even resistance fighters still needed jobs. Nobody was paid for spying on the Nazis or blowing up trains. No matter what Maman was doing for the resistance, she still had to earn money to buy food for herself and Paul.

Mr. Spire pushed his chair over to make room at the table. Mr. Leon was studying a map. He showed Paul the beaches where the Allies would be landing.

"This invasion is just the start," Mr. Leon said. "After the Allies take control of the beaches, more troops and equipment will be coming from England. The Allies will take back our towns and cities. They'll take back Paris. Then they'll battle their way across Europe, all the way to Germany." Mr. Leon ran his finger across the map, and Paul imagined it was magically sweeping the Germans away.

If only beating the Nazis would be that easy.

Paul knew the Nazis would fight back ferociously.

"Do you think the Nazis suspect anything?" Paul asked.

"We hear that Hitler is on vacation in the mountains of Germany," Mr. Leon said.

"I'm afraid his vacation is about to be ruined," Mrs. Bernard quipped.

They all laughed.

But just then the music stopped.

"This is it," Mrs. Bernard said.

Paul expected a voice to say, "The Allied invasion has begun!" or something like that.

But instead, the voice read what sounded like lines from a poem. Something about someone sighing, and violins, and the autumn.

Mr. Leon jumped up. "Yes! That's it!"

Paul looked at Maman.

"It's a message to resistance groups all over France," she said. "It's telling us that the invasion is about to start."

She told him how, all over France, resistance groups had been waiting for this message. "And now they're springing into action," she said. Each group had been given a different assignment by the Allies. Roads to dynamite. Bridges to destroy. Ammunition warehouses to blow up.

"We have another small team here in Le Roc that has been listening for this message," Maman went on. "Their mission is to cut the telephone lines so that local Nazis won't be able to speak to their generals."

Maman put her arm around Paul and hugged him.

"It's happening, Paul. If all goes well, this war — this nightmare — could be over."

Paul's heart rose up.

But then a voice rang from the hallway.

It was Pierre.

"They're back!" Maman said.

But something about the sound of Pierre's voice gave Paul a chill.

They flew out of the room.

He saw Pierre, holding Victor up. There was a trail of blood behind them. Victor's eyes fluttered. Pierre seemed to be using all his strength to support Victor's weight. Paul wondered how he had possibly gotten him back here.

Maman and Mr. Leon rushed over and took hold of Victor.

"What happened?" Maman cried.

Pierre was gasping so much he could barely speak.

"Victor's been shot."

"Where is Marie?" Mr. Leon said, his voice barely a whisper.

Tears poured down Pierre's tough-guy face.

"Marie is dead."

CHAPTER 12

Paul followed Maman and Mr. Spire as they carried Victor to another room.

Paul grabbed Victor's hand. Victor gave his hand a little squeeze, but didn't open his eyes.

"Paul," Maman said gently. "Stay with the others."

Paul tried to go in the room anyway, but Maman started to shut the door. Ellie managed to whoosh in just before she closed it tight.

Paul's whole body was shaking. Somehow, he made it back to the radio room.

Mrs. Bernard took Paul gently by the hand.

"Your mother has helped wounded soldiers before," she said quietly. "Our group has helped rescue nearly fifty Allied pilots who crashed around Le Roc over the years. She knows what to do."

Paul sat down at the table, where Pierre was telling Mr. Leon what happened.

"There were two guards in front of the barn, just as we expected," Pierre said. He had his boot off. His ankle was swollen like a melon. It looked broken, or at least very badly sprained.

"We snuck in through a side door. But we didn't realize there was a third soldier in back. As we were leaving, he spotted us. And then they all came after us. Marie got two of them. And I got the third . . . but not before he shot Marie."

Pierre shook his head, tears streaming down his face. "It's my fault. I should have seen him."

"No," Mr. Leon said sternly. "You cannot blame yourself."

"I didn't even know Victor had been shot," he said. "He said nothing. And I hurt my ankle during the fight; I was worrying about myself. But then, after about a mile, I could see that Victor was about to drop. He was shot in the shoulder. It's bad."

Mr. Leon's face looked calm. But his fists were clenched so tightly his knuckles were white.

"Jacques," Pierre said. "There's something else. About the *Nebelwerfers* . . ."

"What?" Mr. Leon said.

"They weren't there. The barn was empty except for some boxes of ammunition. The *Nebelwerfers* must have been moved."

Pierre pulled out a notebook with a swastika on the cover.

"Victor managed to swipe this from a desk. Hopefully it tells us where the weapons are. We planned to go to find them ourselves. But now . . ."

Mr. Leon took the notebook.

"Pierre," he said. "You did everything you could. We have a long night ahead of us. We must gather our strength for what's to come."

Mr. Leon and Mrs. Bernard began to study the notebook that Pierre had brought from the warehouse. Paul looked over Mr. Leon's shoulder. Pierre was right. The notebook was a careful list of all the weapons, with a map showing where they were placed.

"Their code for *Nebelwerfer* is NbW," Mrs. Bernard told them. "Look for that."

They paged through the book.

"There!" Paul cried as Mr. Leon flipped a page.

"Good eye, son," Mr. Leon said. "Looks like they've put them on the cliffs, over the beach."

Maman had said that this nightmare was about to end.

But Paul now wondered if a new one was about to begin.

CHAPTER 13

Paul got Pierre some water and sat with him a moment.

Then he went and stood outside the room where Victor was and waited.

Maman and Mr. Spire came out a few minutes later. Maman's dress was splattered with blood, her face slick with sweat.

"I got the bullet out and stitched the wound," she said. "I gave him some medicine for the pain. He'll be asleep for a few hours at least."

She wrapped an arm around Paul as they walked back to the radio room.

"Maman . . . will he be all right?" Paul asked.

"I've seen much worse," Maman said. "I do think he's going to make it. We'll know more when he wakes up."

Back in the radio room, Mrs. Bernard said she'd go sit with Victor. She called to Pierre. "Come in with me," she said. "I can wrap up your ankle."

With the Nazi notebook in hand, Mr. Leon repeated Pierre's story for Maman and Mr. Spire. He showed them the page with the location of the *Nebelwerfers* on the cliffs.

"We need to get there and destroy them now," he said.

"But how?" Maman asked. "I ride my bicycle on those roads every day. The road to the beach is blocked off. They have guards posted near all the paths that lead to the cliffs. They've blocked everything off with barbed wire."

Paul peered over Mr. Leon's shoulder at the map once again. He pictured the exact spot where it said *NbW* — a grassy field on the cliffs overlooking the beach.

"I know how to get there without the roads," Paul blurted. "There's a way to cut through the hedgerows, cross these woods, and then climb up over a fence."

Mr. Spire and Mr. Leon looked at Paul.

"Can you draw us a map?" Mr. Spire asked.

Mr. Leon grabbed a piece of paper and a pencil from the box next to the radio.

They watched as Paul started to sketch it out.

But he'd barely gotten started when he realized there was no way he could put his route on paper. There were too many twists and turns, too many secret cuts in the bushes that only Paul — or Gerard — would be able to see.

He put the pencil down.

"I can't draw it or tell you," Paul said. "I need to be able to see where I'm going."

Three sets of eyes stared at him.

"I'll go there. I'll show you."

"No, Paul," Mr. Leon said, putting his hand on Paul's head. "No boy should do anything like this."

Paul knew that was right.

And no eleven-year-old boy should have his papa behind barbed wire. No eleven-year-old boy should see his teacher shot. No eleven-year-old boy should have his best friend taken in the night.

Paul looked at Maman. Their eyes locked. She gave Paul a nod.

"I'll take him," Maman said to Mr. Leon.

"Anna, no. You're the only one who will be able to help Victor if he takes a turn for the worse," Mr. Spire said. "I would go. But this leg . . ."

Mr. Leon sat quietly for what seemed like a very long time.

Finally he stood up.

"Paul," he said. "We leave in five minutes."

CHAPTER 14

JUNE 6, 1944
JUST AFTER MIDNIGHT

The night was very dark, with thick clouds covering the stars. They walked along the paths Paul knew so well. The night was so quiet and peaceful it was impossible to imagine what was ahead. Those ships must already be gathered in the channel, packed with soldiers. Mr. Leon said there might be close to 150,000 men, not only from America and England but Canada and Greece and other countries, too.

Paul thought of what it must be like for those soldiers, riding through the choppy waters in the dark. Would they get seasick? Paul had, the one time he went on a boat ride on the channel.

And what would happen when they got to the beaches?

The boats wouldn't be able to bring them all the way in to the land, Mr. Leon had explained. They would have to get off their boats at least a hundred yards from the beach. They would wade ashore in the freezing water, carrying their guns and supplies.

Paul tried not to think of those Nazi machine guns and cannons poking out from the cliffs, like hungry beasts waiting for their prey.

So instead, he thought of the question he'd been meaning to ask Mr. Leon since he arrived at the castle.

"Mr. Leon," he whispered. "What about that burned body they found near the tower?"

He glanced at Mr. Leon, and to his surprise his teacher wore a faint smile.

"We made it up," he said, stepping over a fallen

branch. "The burned body was a lie, a trick. Pierre wrote up a report in the police department to make it appear official.

"And it worked. Nobody came to the castle," Mr. Leon went on. He looked at Paul. "Until you showed up."

"And what about the dragon?" Paul asked, pointing to a gap in a big bush they needed to pass through. "Do you think about it when you're at the castle?"

Mr. Leon actually slept at the castle, Maman had said.

"I do," Mr. Leon said. "Quite a bit. But not in the way you might think. In the legend, the dragon protects the castle. And when there was a war, the people of Le Roc would rush to the castle for safety."

Paul thought about this. So this old castle had always been a place where people could hide from danger.

"I haven't been to the tower," Mr. Leon continued. "It seems ready to crumble apart. But I've looked up there plenty of times. I haven't seen any glowing eyes, or heard any whooshing wings. To tell you the truth, though, I wouldn't mind if I did. It's lonely in that castle when I'm sleeping there at night. It's nice to think that there's something watching over me. Watching over all of us."

Paul nodded. He liked that idea, too.

They chatted quietly for another couple minutes, until the smell of salt water tickled Paul's nose. They were getting closer to the beach.

It was time to stop talking. This was where most of the Nazis lived, and where Stroop had his headquarters. They crept along, zigzagging their way to the cliffs. There were Nazi guards patrolling the streets, but they looked relaxed. Some talked and joked.

To them this was just a regular night. Paul thought of Hitler, sleeping peacefully, with no idea of what was about to happen.

Paul led Mr. Leon over a stone wall, down a weedy path, and through another hedgerow. On the other side, the Nazis had put up barbed wire. But Mr. Leon put on thick leather gloves and took out a pair of large wire cutters. He pulled and cut the twisted, sharp-pointed wire without shredding his skin.

They hiked up a steep hill, and then there they were.

Ten deadly *Nebelwerfers* lined up in a row.

CHAPTER 15

They didn't look very evil. They were dull gray, with six stubby rocket tubes gathered into a bundle and mounted onto a trailer with very large tires. Each was the size of a small tractor.

Paul and Mr. Leon spotted a Nazi soldier nearby, leaning against a tree, smoking a cigarette.

Mr. Leon picked up a rock. At first Paul thought he was going to throw it at the soldier. But instead, Mr. Leon threw it in the other direction, into the woods.

The rock hit with a loud crack. He quickly

picked up another one, and threw it toward the same spot. And then a third and a fourth. The four rocks hitting sounded like the footsteps of a very large person.

Which was the idea.

The guard tossed his cigarette and headed over to investigate, gripping his machine gun.

Mr. Leon and Paul waited until the guard was out of sight and scurried over.

Mr. Leon took a quick look at the *Nebelwerfers*. "They're loaded," he said.

Even if the Nazis weren't expecting the Allied invasion tonight, they were prepared for an attack. Paul could see the round tips of the rockets sticking out of the ends of the launching tubes.

Mr. Leon had already cut the yellow cake of C-3 into small pieces. In the low light, the pieces almost looked like madeleines.

They were each going to plant the C-3 in five *Nebelwerfers*. Mr. Leon gave Paul six pieces of C-3, in case he dropped one.

Heart pounding, Paul reached into a barrel on the first *Nebelwerfer*. He felt like he was sticking his hand down the throat of a serpent; he half expected it to get chomped off.

He moved down the row, quickly sticking a piece of the C-3 in each one. In moments he was finished. And so was Mr. Leon.

They had done it! Now, when the Nazis tried to fire them at the Allies, these deadly weapons would be blown to pieces.

Paul felt almost weak with relief.

Within the hour, they'd be safe at the castle, safe and sound. Maybe Victor would be awake.

They were creeping back across the field when the sky filled with the sound of a distant whine.

Paul knew the noise all too well: A plane was coming across the channel.

But this wasn't one plane. Paul looked up. Hundreds of large planes were flying toward them, crowded so close together it seemed their striped wings were touching. They were larger than the bombers Paul was used to seeing.

It had to be the paratroopers!

Excitement rose up in Paul, but it quickly turned to dread. Because now the Nazis knew that the Allies were attacking them.

A siren blared.

Explosions roared from the cliffs as the Germans' big cannons — antiaircraft guns — blasted at the planes.

And now there were Nazi soldiers everywhere, even popping up out of the ground. Paul realized

he and Mr. Leon were near the entrance to an underground bunker. Soldiers rose up, like enormous ants boiling out of the dirt.

Paul looked around in horror. There was no way they could escape now.

Mr. Leon reached into his bag. He pulled out what looked like a black apple.

It was a grenade.

"We need to get these soldiers away from here," he said. "I'm going to try to get one of those *Nebelwerfers* to blow. Get ready to hit the dirt and cover your ears."

He pulled the pin from the top of the grenade and tossed it. It landed in front of one of the *Nebelwerfers*.

"Get down, Paul!" Mr. Leon cried.

Paul threw himself to the ground and pressed his hands to his ears as the grenade exploded.

KABOOM!

But that was just the beginning.

The air seemed to shatter as one of the *Nebelwerfers* blew apart.

KABOOM!

It worked! The grenade must have triggered the C-3!

Soldiers scattered, clearing the way for Mr. Leon and Paul to rush back toward the hedgerow.

But now came a new sound, an explosion from the sky.

Paul looked up in horror and saw a plane in flames. It must have been hit by one of the Nazi antiaircraft guns farther down the cliffs. Paratroopers were leaping out of the burning plane. Some of their parachutes opened.

Many did not.

The plane went into a death spiral, flames shooting from the nose and the tail. It was coming in their direction.

"Run, Paul!" Mr. Leon cried.

Paul ran wildly, snapping his head back to watch the plane as it swooped and spiraled. The gagging stench of burning metal and melting rubber seared Paul's eyes and nose.

No matter how fast he ran, no matter in what

direction, that plane was coming right at him. It was like a gigantic, burning wasp.

Paul quickly lost track of Mr. Leon. He was on his own now.

He looked up, fully expecting the plane to fall on top of him.

Something very hard smacked Paul on the head — a plane wheel or a hunk of metal, maybe. His skull felt like it had been cracked open. Blinding pain exploded behind his eyes. Paul dropped to his knees and melted into the ground.

The burning wreckage whizzed within inches of him, sailed over the edge of the cliff, and crashed onto the beach below.

A little voice whispered, *Get up! Get up!*

But Paul couldn't move. He fell hard into a kind of throbbing, nightmarish sleep.

When he finally opened his eyes, hours later, it was getting light. He was dazed, and his head still hurt. He was on a rocky ledge, looking over the beach. It took him a long moment to remember what had happened, and to notice that he wasn't by himself. There was a Nazi soldier standing over him.

Paul raised his arms in surrender.

He'd been captured.

CHAPTER 16

5:50 A.M.

The soldier — he looked so young Paul wondered if he was even eighteen — held his hand out toward Paul. It took Paul a moment to understand: He was offering to help Paul to his feet.

"Danke," Paul said.

Paul had barely realized he knew that German word.

Thank you.

Their eyes met. The soldier didn't look like a

cruel Nazi. He looked like a kid, someone Paul and Gerard might have wanted to play soccer with.

But then the young soldier suddenly stood up straight. He clicked the heels of his black boots together and threw his arm straight out in front of him — a Nazi salute. Paul whirled around and saw a furious-looking Nazi officer.

The man's face was red with rage. He shoved the young soldier so hard the young man stumbled and almost fell. And then the officer stood over Paul, so close that Paul could smell the man's sour sweat.

"What are you doing here?" the Nazi bellowed. "Nobody is allowed in this area! It is strictly forbidden." He reminded Paul of Stroop — the animal glint in his eye, the knife-sharp edge of his voice. How Paul could sense how much he enjoyed this, that he had the power to make people feel terrified.

The Nazi reached over and roughly searched Paul's pockets. He pulled out something small.

Paul's blood turned to ice. The C-3 — that

extra slab that Mr. Leon had given him. Paul had forgotten that he still had it.

The Nazi held it up and studied it carefully. His eyes narrowed to needle slits. He knew exactly what it was, Paul could see.

Paul turned to bolt, but the Nazi clamped his hand on Paul's arm. Paul tried to jerk away, but the hand gripped him like a metal claw.

The Nazi shouted out, and two other soldiers rushed toward them.

Paul's heart filled with terror as he thought of what would happen next. They would drag him to some dark dungeon, and make him tell them where he had gotten the C-3. Paul's mind flashed with knives, with flames, all the terrible ways the Nazis would hurt him so he'd tell them his secrets — about the resistance, Mr. Leon, and Maman.

Thunder rumbled, as though Paul's fear was tearing open the sky.

Paul glanced out over the English Channel. Through the thick fog, he could see small flashes of orange.

There was a faint whistling sound that got louder and louder and louder:

Sssssssssssssssss.

Seconds later,

Kaboom!

An explosion rocked the ground. Both Paul and the Nazi fell into the grass. Paul rolled away from him as black, billowing smoke blinded him. Everything around Paul seemed to go quiet.

He coughed, and tears poured from his eyes. The smoke cleared, and Paul saw that the Nazi who'd grabbed him was still on the ground, deathly still. That blast had killed him.

Paul scrambled to his feet. He still had no idea what was happening, but this was his chance to get away from here. He started to run.

But then it hit him . . . that thundering sound. The bright orange flashes through the fog. The explosion.

The Allied ships were here!

The thunder roared again.

Sssssssssssssssss. Kaboom!

The Allies were firing from their battleships,

Paul realized. They must be trying to crush the Nazi defenses — the machine guns and cannons that were lined up on the cliffs. The Allies wanted to clear the way before their soldiers poured onto the beaches.

But if Paul didn't get out of here now, those Allied battleships were going to crush him, too.

CHAPTER 17

6:30 A.M.

Paul had to find somewhere to hide. But where?

Off to the side he saw a big hedgerow, behind a pile of rocks. The rocks might just protect him from the blasts. The hedgerow could keep him hidden from the Nazis.

Paul rushed over. The tall, prickly bush looked as solid as a wall. But of course Paul knew better. He quickly found an opening, a place where the branches grew apart.

His heart was racing. But he closed his eyes and imagined that Gerard was sitting next to him.

It had suddenly grown very quiet. The Allied guns had stopped firing.

Paul opened his eyes, and stared ahead at the sea with wonder.

The fog had disappeared. And so, it seemed, had the English Channel.

All Paul could see now were ships — thousands and thousands of them. There were ships and boats of all sizes and shapes. Above them, in the sky, floated hundreds of huge silver balloons. Paul wasn't sure, but he thought maybe those were meant to keep enemy planes from swooping down to attack the ships.

The boats stretched out as far as Paul could see, in every direction.

Mr. Leon's voice rang through Paul's mind.

The largest invasion by sea in the history of the world.

And unlike the legend of the dragon, these words were true.

Paul saw it all with his own eyes. If only Gerard were here to see it with him.

The ships sped forward.

Why weren't the Nazis attacking back? Where were the cannons and machine guns that lined the cliffs?

Paul's heart rose.

Had those Allied battleships destroyed all the cannons and machine guns? Were the Nazis slinking away or huddled in their bunkers?

The first of the ships were just a few hundred yards from the shore now. Paul pulled the branches open a little more so he could see better. He fixed his gaze on one of the smaller boats. It was still very far away. But Paul could see that it was packed with soldiers, rows of men in green. The boat rose up and down as it plowed forward through the rough waves. Paul imagined how water must be spraying into the boat, soaking the men. They must be freezing.

And scared.

The boat stopped when it was still maybe two hundred yards away from shore. That was the closest the boats could come, Paul realized. The Germans had lined the beach with giant metal and wooden stakes. There were also under-ground bombs — mines — buried under the sand, Paul had heard.

Paul leaned forward so his face was out of the hedge. He watched as the front of that boat was lowered, and men slid into the water that rose to their chests.

They were quickly joined by other men, from other boats. They pushed their way forward, through the choppy sea.

"Come on! Come on!" Paul wanted to shout.

And that's when the German guns came to life.

Cannons blasted from the cliffs.

Kaboom!

Machine guns roared.

Brrrrrrrrrrrttttt! Brrrrrrrrrrrrttttt!

Paul froze in horror as men were mowed down by the dozens. By the hundreds.

There was so much smoke that the ships seemed to disappear. But he heard the explosions as the ships were hit. He saw the flames.

And the men.

More and more of them were in the water now, making their way toward the beach. They pushed through the spray of machine gun fire. Some fell back and sank into the bloody water. But others made it to the beach.

And then?

There was no place for them to hide from the nonstop spray of machine gun fire.

Soon the beach was covered with bodies. Men cried out for help. Red, foaming waves crashed onto the shore.

Something inside Paul's mind seemed to snap.

His eyes stopped seeing. His ears stopped hearing.

He leaned back and the branches seemed to wrap themselves around his body.

The leaves seemed to put gentle fingers over his face.

The hedgerow seemed to grow and grow, surrounding Paul like the walls of a castle.

Paul sat there, praying for this nightmare to end.

—

"Son? Son?"

Paul's eyes snapped open.

He was looking into the face of a man with very dark skin. A soldier, wearing a helmet. He gently grabbed hold of Paul, like he was a wounded baby deer. And he pulled him out of the hedgerow.

Paul saw the American flag patch on the arm of his uniform.

The soldier helped Paul to his feet and waited a minute.

"Okay?" he said, raising his eyebrows.

Paul nodded, though he wasn't sure what the man meant.

The soldier gave him a pat on the arm and hurried off.

Paul had no idea how much time had passed. He felt dazed. But the battle was still raging. Machine guns still roared. The cannons exploded. But somehow those Americans had made it up here.

So all was not lost.

Paul refused to look at the channel or the beaches.

He just wanted to get back to Maman.

The thick smoke made it hard to see, but Paul could run this route with his eyes closed.

Nobody tried to stop him.

CHAPTER 18

```
THREE DAYS LATER
JUNE 9, 1944
CASTLE LE ROC
3:00 P.M.
```

Paul and Maman were alone in the radio room, listening to the news on the radio.

"This is the BBC, London, reporting from the Allied invasion of France. Our landings have been successful and more troops and supplies are on the way. Fighting continues, but Allied forces continue to take control . . ."

In the distance they could hear the sounds of Allied planes, and bombs falling farther to the south. But for now they felt safe in the castle. Victor was asleep. He was feeling stronger, but it was still a struggle for him to stand for more than a few minutes at a time. Of course Ellie was watching over him, sitting at the edge of the mattress.

Pierre and Mrs. Bernard had gone home. So now it was just Maman and Paul, alone. Like it used to be. Except not exactly. Now they had no secrets between them.

They listened to the radio a while longer. But then Maman turned the radio off.

"I think we need a little quiet," she said.

Paul agreed. The silence helped soothe his head, which still ached from when he got hit on the night of the invasion.

He got up and looked out the window.

He wasn't looking for paratroopers anymore. Now he was looking for Mr. Leon. His teacher had never returned from the cliffs that night. Nobody knew what had happened.

Maman came up behind him. They both stood

there a moment, looking out into the gray afternoon.

"Help me get some water," she said, waving for Paul to follow her outside. They kept buckets placed outside the walls to catch rainwater to drink and wash with.

The afternoon was chilly, raining on and off. But it felt good to be out in the fresh air. He and Maman each picked up a wooden bucket.

Suddenly they heard running footsteps.

Paul turned and saw three Nazi soldiers heading toward them. In front was Stroop.

Paul and Maman froze, but then Maman put down her bucket. She stood up very straight, and managed to hide the fear that must have been gripping her by the throat.

"Search the castle," Stroop ordered the men, who strode through the castle door.

He walked over and stood very close to Maman. His eyes flicked across her face.

"Where is he?" he asked in an icy voice.

"I'm sorry, sir," Maman said calmly. "Who are you looking for?"

Mr. Leon, of course.

"You know who," Stroop answered. "The resistance leader who somehow rose from the dead."

Paul's mind was swirling. How did Stroop find them? How did he know Mr. Leon hadn't died in the river that day?

Maman stepped back. "I have no idea who you are speaking of."

Without a blink, Stroop gave Maman a vicious smack across the face.

And there it was, that cruel smile.

Paul gripped his bucket. And with all the strength he could muster, he lifted it up, and slammed it against Stroop's head. The Nazi fell to the ground, dripping wet and bleeding.

Paul and Maman took off around the side of the castle. Stroop shouted after them, and bullets flew through the air.

Paul looked around, searching for a hedgerow to hide in, a secret path that would lead them to safety. But he didn't know the land on this side of the castle very well. It was Maman who gripped his hand and led him around a corner, then through a doorway. They heard gunshots echoing from inside the castle, and Paul's knees went weak as he thought of Victor.

But he and Maman kept running. They rushed up a narrow stone staircase, higher and higher, higher and higher, their boots echoing on the stones.

They ran until they could go no higher. They had reached the castle tower.

It was small and dark. Paul and Maman huddled together.

Seconds later Stroop appeared, panting.

He stared at them, gripping his gun. His face was smeared with blood. But again, there was that smile, jagged like a crack in a frozen puddle.

"Why are you doing this?" Maman said, stepping in front of Paul. "The Allies are here. The war will soon be over. Haven't you caused enough misery? Enough suffering? When will you stop?"

Maman's voice was clear and strong.

For a split second, Paul thought he might have glimpsed the tiniest flicker of doubt on Stroop's face. But then Stroop lifted his gun.

Maman grabbed hold of Paul. And at that same moment, a great winged creature swooped into the tower.

With a piercing shriek it attacked the Nazi.

"What is this?" Stroop screamed. "Help me! Help me!"

The creature clawed at Stroop's hands until he dropped the gun. It hissed and shrieked and flapped its wings.

Whoosh! Whoosh!

Stroop staggered back in terror until he hit the tower wall.

The old wall had somehow held itself together for a thousand years, through centuries of wars and storms and endless dark nights. But it was at this moment that the wall finally crumbled.

The wall seemed to fall apart in slow motion, stones tumbling outward.

Stroop teetered on the edge. Then he was gone, too.

The Nazi's screams rose through the air and Paul covered his ears. He had heard enough deathly sounds.

Moments later Victor appeared in the doorway, breathless, holding his gun.

He rushed over to Maman and Paul, moving with great speed for someone who had recently been shot.

"What happened?"

The answer landed at their feet.

The brave winged creature looked up at them with her gleaming gold eyes.

"Coo-roo, coo-roo."

CHAPTER 19

"When's he coming, Papa? When's he coming!?"

Paul smiled. His six-year-old son, Jacques, was as excited as he was. They were having a special visitor today, someone who Paul hadn't seen since the war.

Paul's wife, Valerie, scooped Jacques up. "Let's go to Grandma and Grandpa's," she said to him.

"Daddy needs some time alone with his old friend."

Paul walked to the porch and watched them disappear down the winding road.

"Don't let your friend leave without meeting me!" Jacques shrieked.

Paul smiled and sat down on the porch.

He breathed in the familiar smells of sweet grass and apples and that hint of salt from the sea. There was nothing better.

Paul had traveled some. He and Valerie had visited Victor in Texas twice.

But Le Roc was his home.

It had changed in the fifteen years since the war.

Most of the town had been destroyed in those terrible weeks after D-Day. The Allies dropped thousands of bombs to try to stop the Nazi troops, to destroy their supplies and weapons. They tried to spare the people of Normandy. But by the time the Nazis finally fled, thousands of French people were dead.

It wasn't until the following September that World War II finally ended.

Paul stood up and looked down the road again. He checked his watch.

This special visitor would arrive any minute.

What would it be like to be together again after all this time? Would seeing him bring back all those years of fear and pain?

Even now, memories came back to Paul out of nowhere — those men dying on the beach on D-Day, the bombs raining down as he and Maman huddled together in their basement.

But of course there were happy memories, too.

Like when Mr. Leon finally returned to the Castle Le Roc. He'd been injured in an Allied bombing, but somehow made it back. He was bruised and bloodied but amazed to hear the story of Ellie and Stroop. It was a story far better than any legend of a dragon.

Paul smiled to himself, thinking of how much Jacques loved that story. There was only one story he loved more. It was the story about how

Papa — Jacques's grandfather — got home after the war.

"You really walked for four months, Grandpa?" Jacques would ask, stroking his grandfather's snow-white beard. "Didn't your feet hurt?"

"I had to get home to my boy," he'd say, glancing at Paul. "And to your grandmother," he'd add, smiling at Maman. "For them I would have walked to the moon and back."

Jacques would lean forward. "Grandpa," he'd whisper. "You can't walk to the moon."

Paul had tried not to think too much about the war after Papa came home. Life moved forward. Papa got stronger after his years in the prison camp. They rebuilt their house. Time passed. Paul went to college and met Valerie. They moved back here and had Jacques. Paul tried his best to forget the past.

But then, a month ago, the past arrived in a letter for Paul.

My old friend, it began. *My name is Gerry Goldman, but you will remember me as Gerard Drey . . .*

Paul's hands had started to shake when he read that, and Valerie had to finish reading the letter for him.

"My parents were murdered by the Nazis," Valerie had read aloud. *"But the day before my parents were arrested, they managed to get me into the hands of the Le Roc resistance."*

Into the hands of Maman, Mr. Leon, and the others, Paul would learn. They'd rescued Gerard and three other Jewish children from Le Roc. They'd hidden them at the castle. And then somehow they'd gotten them to a village in the mountains where dozens of Jewish children were hidden throughout the war.

Maman had never told this to Paul — it was the one secret she'd never shared. She later explained it to Paul, tears brimming in her eyes. "We were never sure if Gerard survived the war."

So many Jewish people didn't.

But Gerard had made it. And after the war, his father's cousins tracked him down and took him to America.

As Gerard's letter explained, he went on to live

a happy life. Over time, though, his memories of his childhood in France had dimmed. The loss of his family was so painful. Like Paul, he'd tried his best to forget those dark years.

"But I've never forgotten you, Paul."

This visitor Paul was waiting for now — it was Gerard.

Paul paced back and forth on the porch until the sound of a car sent him rushing to the steps.

And at last, there he was: his best friend. Gerard was tall. His curls had gone straight. But there was that lopsided smile. They stood on the porch and stared at each other, tears running down their faces. Within seconds, the long years between them disappeared.

They talked and talked, and then Maman and Papa and Jacques and Valerie came home. And they talked some more.

They told Gerard all about Victor, the castle, and the death of Stroop. Gerard showed them pictures of his wife and daughters. Valerie cooked lunch and they polished off a whole plate of madeleine cookies, still Maman's favorites.

And then, when the plates were scraped clean, Jacques grabbed Gerard's hand and said, "Let's go outside!"

Jacques dragged Gerard past Maman and Papa and Valerie and out they went into the sunny afternoon. Paul started to follow them, but then he remembered something. He went to his closet and opened a box. He took out a treasure he'd been saving for exactly this day, should it ever come.

That old brown soccer ball.

It turned out that Boris, the old leatherworker, was in the resistance, too.

Paul went outside and kicked the ball to Gerard. He stopped it with his foot and stared at it like it was another long-lost friend.

He tapped it gently to Jacques, who kicked the ball with all his might.

Thwack!

It sailed through the air and disappeared into the hedgerow.

"I lost it!" Jacques cried, a worried look on his face.

"No, you didn't," Paul said.

Because of course Paul had learned that many things could be found, if you knew where to look.

You could find a safe place, inside the walls of a ruined castle.

You could find courage, inside a heart pounding with fear.

You could find hope, coming across a foggy sea.

Jacques rushed up and down the hedgerow, biting his lip nervously as he peered inside the twisted branches.

Finally he pointed. "I see it," he exclaimed. He pulled the ball out, hugged it tight, and then dropped it on the ground. He gave it a powerful kick, and the ball went sailing across the yard.

Paul looked at Gerard and smiled, wiping away his last happy tear of the day.

"Race you," Paul said to his old friend.

And they both took off through the bright green grass.

KEEP READING!

Read why Lauren Tarshis wrote about
D-Day and learn more facts about the
largest sea invasion in history!

WRITING ABOUT D-DAY

Dear Readers,

This past July, my husband and I stood on one of the most beautiful beaches I've ever seen. It seemed to stretch out forever, miles of white sand where kids were making castles and dogs were chasing balls.

Standing there, under a bright-blue sky, it was almost impossible to imagine that this was the same blood-soaked beach — code-named Omaha — I had been learning about as I researched this book. I tried to imagine what it had been like for the American soldiers who attempted to come ashore on D-Day. I had read so many of their interviews and letters that

I could almost hear their voices whispering to me as I walked the beach.

Right here is where my friend died.

Over there is where a boat filled with soldiers exploded.

The whole ocean seemed to be filled with blood.

More than three thousand men were hurt or killed on that beach. And truly, their spirits seemed to be all around. Being at that beach and thinking about all those who died broke my heart.

But being in Normandy was inspiring. Because the people there continue to honor the soldiers — American, British, Canadian, and others — who risked and lost their lives to free the French people from the Nazis. In almost every town there is a museum, or a statue, or a memorial. There are streets named after American soldiers. I will never forget my day at the cemetery that sits right above Omaha Beach. There, in simple graves marked with Christian crosses and Jewish Stars of David, lie 9,385 of the men killed on D-Day.

Writing about D-Day was often sad. And extremely difficult. Because of course it's not just the story of one day, one battle.

It's the story of one of the biggest, most complicated

and tragic events in all of history: World War II. My books are historical fiction, which means the facts are true and the characters are fictional.

But as I created Paul's world, I wanted to give you a real idea of what it must have been like to live in a French town taken over by the Nazis. I based all of Paul's experiences on those of real people I discovered in my research: Finding a paratrooper in a tree. Hiding an Allied soldier. Having a mom in the resistance. Coping with the fear that a Jewish friend might be taken in the night. Having a very creepy castle in your town. These are all experiences that real kids in Normandy had during World War II.

And trying to weave all that together into an interesting story was hard (just ask my super-kind editor, Katie, and my husband and kids, who kept encouraging me, and my dog, Roy, who, as always, was by my side at all times). I kept writing drafts. Then starting again . . . and starting yet again. And eating bags of pretzels and bowls of ice cream, and starting again.

The story just wasn't working . . . until the pigeon.

I actually met a pigeon during that summer trip to Normandy. I was doing work on a little terrace. And this fat pigeon kept coming to visit me. It was very beautiful and there was something very smart and fascinating and funny about it. I even spent time trying to get a picture of it, which I finally did.

The pigeon that inspired the character of Ellie

That pigeon found its way into my heart. But I wasn't thinking about it as I was writing all those drafts. Until one day it came to me: carrier pigeons! I remembered that pigeons were a HUGE part of World War II. The Allies used 250,000 pigeons to carry messages. Back in 1944, the clever birds were often far more reliable than a radio or a telephone.

Ellie enabled me to add a little bit of lightness to the dark story of war, Nazis, and the resistance. And once I added her, the book seemed to work.

I hope you agree. And even more, I hope reading my one small story makes you hungry to learn more on your own.

Au revoir (that's good-bye in French),

The author visits with D-Day survivor Denise Voydie, 97, and friends, in the village of Graignes, France

SOME QUESTIONS THAT MIGHT BE ON YOUR MIND

Did D-Day end World War II?

No. But it was a huge step that helped the Allies on their path to victory over the Nazis. The invasion was part of a larger mission called "Operation Overlord." The goal of the mission: free Europe from the Nazis. On D-Day, the Allies succeeded in smashing through Nazi defenses.

In the weeks following the invasion, the Allies poured hundreds of thousands of troops, weapons, tanks, and supplies into Europe. By September, most of France was free. But the fighting and killing went on and on, and not only in the countries around France. Some of the biggest battles in World War II happened far to the east, in and around Russia.

And Germany wasn't the Allies' only enemy. As the Nazis were conquering countries in Europe, Japan was invading countries in Asia and islands in the Pacific Ocean. There were battles not only in Europe but also throughout Asia, the Pacific Ocean, and northern and eastern Africa.

The war finally ended in September of 1945. More than 60 million people died in battles and from diseases connected to the hardships of war.

How did the Allies keep D-Day a secret from the Germans?

D-Day was doomed to fail unless the Germans were taken by surprise. During the year of planning, the planners kept the time and location of the invasion a total secret. Even Allied soldiers didn't know exactly where they were going until the morning before. The Allies also tricked the Nazis. They wanted to make the Germans believe that the invasion was going to happen farther south. In the months before, they created fake coded radio messages they knew the Nazis would hear. They created fake airplanes and blow-up rubber tanks that made it seem they were about to attack farther north. All of the secrecy and tricks worked.

Is it true that Jewish children were hidden from the Nazis?

Between 1939 and 1945, the Nazis murdered 6 million Jewish people in Europe. Most were forced from their homes and sent to concentration camps, large prisons where they were worked to death, shot, or killed with poisoned gas. A small number of Jewish people were saved by heroic neighbors and others who hid them and helped them escape. They did this even though they and their families would have been killed or sent to concentration camps if they had been caught. The story of Gerard is inspired by several stories I read about real French Jewish children who survived the Holocaust.

Is Le Roc a real place?

Le Roc is a fictional village. But it was inspired by the many I visited while researching this book. These villages are quiet and beautiful. They are crisscrossed with hedgerows, which Normandy is famous for. The hedgerows were planted centuries ago to be walls between fields and pastures, to keep horses and cows from escaping, and to help keep water from flooding the fields.

During the war, the hedgerows caused problems for the Allies. Paratroopers and gliders crashed into them. The Nazis used them as places to hide before sneak attacks. As I explored Normandy, I kept imagining how a kid like Paul might have discovered secret paths and openings in the hedgerows. I knew they would be an important part of the story.

Did many French people die during Operation Overlord?

Yes. The French suffered terribly in the Allied bombings in the weeks that followed D-Day.

Despite the losses caused by the bombings, most French people felt enormous gratitude toward the Allies. They hung American flags in front of their houses. They forged lifelong friendships with the paratroopers they rescued from trees, or the troops they sheltered in their homes. Overall, the French people understood that men from across oceans risked their lives to save France from the Nazis. And they have never forgotten.

People from Normandy welcoming Allied troops in the weeks after D-Day

SOME VEHICLES USED DURING OPERATION OVERLORD

British Horsa Glider
These engineless planes were towed across the ocean, and then landed noiselessly in Normandy. They carried troops, weapons, trucks, and other equipment.

DUKW
Part truck, part boat, these vehicles could float through the water and drive up onto shore.

American Jeep
The Jeep you know today was first created for American soldiers during World War II.

Spitfire
The most common Allied airplane of World War II. This one has Canadian markings.

US Landing Craft, Vehicle and Personnel
There were different kinds of landing crafts built for D-Day. Some carried tanks. This one carried troops and smaller vehicles.

Motorcycle
Motorcycles were used by both the Nazis and the Allies throughout the war.

A TIMELINE OF D-DAY

D-Day was the largest invasion by sea in the history of the world. In one day, approximately 150,000 soldiers, mostly from the United States, England, and Canada (the Allies), crossed the English Channel in thousands of ships and planes to attack over 50,000 German troops in Normandy, an area in the northwest of France.

Their plan was to land at five beaches along France's north coast in a region called Normandy. The invasion took months of planning, and up until the last minute, many thought it would fail.

They were wrong.

Here are the key events of June 5–6, 1944:

JUNE 5, 4:00 A.M.:
Plans Become Final

The person in charge of the invasion was United States General Dwight D. Eisenhower, and he had to make the final decision to say "go" to the invasion. The weather was stormy. But Eisenhower decided that the invasion would begin the next morning, during a short break in the bad weather. He wrote a letter that was read to all troops. He told them, "The eyes of the world are upon you."

General Dwight D. Eisenhower gives the order to troops before the invasion. "Full victory — nothing else."

JUNE 5, 6:00 A.M. TO 10:00 P.M.:
Ships Gather in the Sea

Nearly seven thousand ships, packed with troops, weapons, tanks, and supplies, all gather at Area Z, a huge meeting place in the middle of the English Channel.

Allied landing craft in the English Channel on their way to the beaches of Normandy

JUNE 5, 10:00 P.M.:
Paratroopers Board Planes

The night before the invasion, 13,100 American paratroopers board their transport planes at bases across England. They are members of the US 82nd and 101st Airborne Divisions. Each man is carrying more than a hundred pounds of equipment.

Paratroopers in a plane just before taking off for the D-Day invasion. The soldier in the middle holds the letter from General Eisenhower.

JUNE 5, 1944, 11:15 P.M.: The Resistance Is Called

A powerful radio station in London — the BBC — sends out a coded message to resistance groups across France. It is a line from a poem by a man named Paul Verlaine. The resistance groups begin blowing up trains and train tracks, cutting power and telephone cables, and destroying important roads. These missions were designed to keep more German soldiers and equipment away from the beaches at Normandy.

JUNE 6, 1944, 12:02 A.M.: First Paratroopers Arrive

The 13,100 men of the 82nd and 101st Airborne Divisions jumped into the darkness behind enemy lines. Their job was to block German soldiers and tanks from helping the Nazis push back the Allied invasion, to capture roads to the beaches, and to establish bridges over two important rivers. Men from the British 6th Airborne Division, along with some Canadian troops, had the job of trying to destroy bridges to stop Germans from getting to the beaches.

JUNE 6, 3:00 A.M.: Hitler Sleeps

German leader Adolf Hitler goes to bed in his mountain home. Even though the German military had already received reports of a possible Allied invasion at Normandy, Hitler was not told. His closest aides were too afraid of being wrong or displeasing him. This delay will cost the Germans dearly — Hitler would sleep on for nine hours!

JUNE 6, 1944, 4:00 A.M.: Gliders Land

Gliders were large, very light planes that could carry four thousand pounds of equipment and soldiers, but had no engines. To get up in the air, a glider had be tugged by a regular military transport plane. It was towed like a kite across the channel. When the plane neared its landing spot, the towrope was released, and the glider would silently swoop down to its secret landing zone.

JUNE 6, 5:50 A.M.: Battleships Blast the Coast at Omaha Beach

American and British gunships start blasting at the German guns on the cliffs overlooking Omaha Beach. Similar attacks take place at the other four D-Day landing beaches.

The British HMS Warspite *firing at the German gun batteries on the coast of Normandy*

JUNE 6, 6:30 A.M.: Allied Troops Hit the Beach

During D-Day, Allied troops landed on the five Normandy beaches. Each beach had been given its own code name: Utah, Omaha, Gold, Juno, and Sword. The Americans arrive first on Utah and Omaha at 6:30 A.M. Over the next ninety minutes, tens of thousands of British and Canadian soldiers land on Gold, Juno, and Sword Beaches.

American troops exit a landing craft and wade ashore at Utah Beach

The News Is Out

England's BBC now broadcasts a clear message to England and the world: "Allied naval forces ... began landing Allied armies this morning on the northern coast of France." Millions of people from around the world had been hoping and praying this announcement would come.

JUNE 6, 10:00 A.M. TO 12:00 NOON: Germany's Generals Panic

German military commanders panic as Hitler sleeps. Finally, at noon, he is awoken and told of the Normandy invasion. He seems happy because, in his mind, hundreds of thousands of Allied soldiers are now in the range of German guns. He does not understand the size and power of the Allied invasion.

JUNE 6, 12:00 NOON TO THE MORNING OF JUNE 7: D-Day Mission Is Complete

The mission is a success, though the cost is high. Approximately 4,400 Allied soldiers died during the invasion. More than ten thousand were injured. Ninety-one percent of Allied troops make it off the beaches on June 6. Over the next two months, the Allies battle to sweep the Nazis from Normandy. On August 25, the Allies free Paris. More than one year later, on September 9, 1945, World War II finally ends.

Injured soldiers after the invasion of Omaha Beach

FURTHER READING

Some books you might enjoy about
D-Day and the Resistance:

D-Day: The Invasion of Normandy, 1944 [The Young Readers Adaptation], by Rick Atkinson, Square Fish; First Square Fish Edition, 2015

Ranger in Time: D-Day: Battle on the Beach, by Kate Messner, Scholastic Inc., 2018

Resistance, by Carla Jablonski & Leland Purvis, First Second, 2010

Resistance, by Jennifer Nielsen, Scholastic Press, 2018

Other I Survived books set during the
World War II era:

SELECTED BIBLIOGRAPHY

Bailout Over Normandy: A Flyboy's Adventures with the French Resistance and Other Escapades in Occupied France, by Ted Fahrenwald, Casemate Publishers, 2012

Band of Brothers, by Stephen Ambrose, Simon & Schuster, 1992

Churchill's Ministry of Ungentlemanly Warfare: The Mavericks Who Plotted Hitler's Defeat, by Giles Milton, Picador, 2016

D-Day: The Invasion of Normandy, 1944 [The Young Readers Adaptation], by Rick Atkinson, Square Fish; First Square Fish Edition, 2015

D-Day Through French Eyes: Normandy 1944, by Mary Louise Roberts, University of Chicago Press, 2014

The Jedburghs: The Secret History of the Allied Special Forces, France 1944, by Will Irwin, PublicAffairs, a member of The Perseus Group, 2005

The Longest Day: The Classic Epic of D-Day, by Cornelius Ryan, Simon & Schuster, 1994

The Secret Agent's Pocket Manual, by Stephen Bull, Osprey Publishing UK, 2017

The Secret War: Spies, Ciphers, and Guerrillas, 1939–1945, by Jack Olsen, Harper Perennial; Reprint Edition, 2017

ACKNOWLEDGMENTS

As always, many people helped me bring this I Survived book into the world. First, I want to express my enormous gratitude for my editor, Katie Woehr, who offered me her truly unique blend of bracing encouragement, editorial wisdom, and kindness in the face of an unusually challenging writing journey.

During my research trip through Normandy, I had the good fortune to connect with three people who enabled me to walk in the footsteps of my characters. Thank you to Sylvan Kast, guide extraordinaire, for leading my husband, David, and me on an unforgettable trip. His passion and insights informed every part of the story. In particular, Sylvan enabled us to meet Denise Voydie, who welcomed us into her home and shared her childhood memories of the Nazi occupation and D-Day. A third generous new friend, Corinne Le Moignic Capiten, embraced David and me like we were members of her family and guided us through the city of Falaise, which was leveled during the battles that followed D-Day. I am grateful to Bob Kern, who helped plan our research trip, which also included crossing the English Channel.

As always, my husband, David Dreyfuss, was by my side at every step of researching and writing — planning trips, checking facts, reviewing drafts, and writing encouraging notes that greeted me each morning when I staggered out of bed at 4:30 A.M. to work on this book.

And finally, thank you also to my I Survived family: Debra Dorfman, Ellie Berger, Heather Daugherty, Julie Amitie, Carmen Alvarez, Charisse Meloto, Scott Dawson, Colin Anderson, and many others who help these books get into readers' hands.

I SURVIVED

When disaster strikes, heroes are made.

Read the bestselling series by Lauren Tarshis!

SCHOLASTIC

ISURVIVED18

I SURVIVED
TRUE STORIES

REAL KIDS.
REAL DISASTERS.

I Survived True Stories feature riveting narrative non-fiction stories of unimaginable destruction— and, against all odds, survival.

Join the Historians Club at scholastic.com/isurvived